PRESENT CONFLICTS

INSPIRED BY TRUE EVENTS

PHIL-WILL

Back to the world where secrets run deep and loyalty is tested at every turn, Cedric "Chill" James finds himself at the center of a web of betrayal, love, and vengeance. After a violent stabbing leaves him fighting for his life, Chill is forced to confront the unresolved tensions and hidden truths that surround him.

From the strained relationship with his cousin Jamal and the complicated history with Chantel, to the unsettling realization that someone close might have wanted him dead, Chill's recovery is anything but peaceful. As he navigates his way through the emotional minefield of family dynamics and old grudges, he must also come to terms with unexpected fatherhood, commitment and sacrifice.

Present Conflicts is a gripping tale of resilience, trust, and the thin line between love and betrayal. As secrets unfold and the past catches up, the true challenge lies not just in survival, but in uncovering who can be trusted when everyone has something to hide.

Contents

Chapter One

I hate it here...

"Oh, shit. Oh shit!" was all Chill could hear as someone ran towards him. "Are you okay? Can you hear me?"

He could hear the person clearly, above the loud beating of his heart, as he pressed his hand against his abdomen to slow down the bleeding. The person immediately crouched beside him, reaching for his phone as his other hand also pressed against the wound. He was sure he had heard a gunshot.

The stab wound confused him.

"911, what's your emergency?" the dispatcher's voice rang from the phone.

"Y-yeah, I'm at the Holiday Inn in the parking lot. A man here got stabbed—I think it's to his kidney. Lost a lot of blood, and he barely has a pulse," the man said.

Kidney? For fuck's sake. It was the only thing he could give to Di'Vanni—his son, and he was about to lose that too.

There was a bit of noise on the other line. "We have services on the way. Just keep applying pressure."

He hung up after that and looked at Chill, pulling him up. "Hey, keep your eyes open," he said, noticing that Chill was slipping. "Can you keep your hand right here? Is this your car?"

The questions annoyed Chill, but he nodded as the man left him and threw the truck open. He quickly got a towel long enough to wrap around the bleeding.

"I knew I would find something," he said, and Chill grunted in pain when he tightened the knot. "I was a medic in the Army, so trust me a bit. I'm gonna try to apply pressure until the ambulance gets here." He snapped his fingers when Chill's eyes dazed. "You need to keep your eyes open. Try to nod if you can hear me."

Chill tried to nod as he instructed but suddenly felt choked and coughed. The effort sent blood up his throat and out his mouth. He didn't know dying was so painful. Hopefully, Nathan hadn't gone through this much pain.

A while later, they heard an ambulance in the distance speeding towards them, and the man sighed in relief. Chill, on the other hand, believed they must have been on the other street to arrive so quickly.

The vehicle parked right in front of them, the EMTs pulling out a stretcher and strapping Chill to it before hauling him inside.

"What did you say happened here?" one asked the man, a notepad in his hand.

"Heard a gunshot then saw him on the ground holding his side."

The EMT nodded. "You did a great job. We've got it from here."

~~~

Lucky got into the house and immediately headed to the room where Nikki folded the laundry. She didn't look at him.

"Hey," he called, demanding her attention. "Did you make that call for me?"

She nodded. "Yeah, I told her he wasn't going anywhere."

"Cool. Now forget you ever did that."

Nikki frowned. "Why, though? Why you want someone to know Chill's still in town?"

He glared at her. "It's none of your business. Now forget you did that shit or it gon' cost you."

He knew he fucked up, but there was no way anybody could know that he was involved. It was way too risky.

~~~

Jamal scrolled through his phone as he waited at the corner of his usual spot for his fix. He was mad as hell that Chantel still had not called him even after he had asked her to. The way she acted most of the time pissed him off.

His phone screen lit up, and he scowled at the ID. It was an unknown number.

Hesitantly, he answered. "Hello?"

"Hello. Is this Jamal James?"

"Yes. Who is this?" he asked cautiously.

"I'm a nurse at Regional, and Cedric James has you as his emergency contact," the nurse said, and Jamal's eyes widened.

"What? What happened to Chill?!"

"He's been stabbed and badly injured. I believe it is in your best interest to want to come down to say your goodbyes."

Jamal froze in shock, the nurse calling him repeatedly over the line as a small echo at the back of his mind. Chill... Injured... Goodbyes.

He could hear his heart pounding against his ribcage as he brought the phone to his ear. "Yes, I'm here. I'm on my way. Thank you."

He quickly got back to the apartment, not stopping until Dez stepped in front of him, holding a cigarette.

"Mal, what's up?" he asked with concern, and Jamal shrugged his hand off of him.

"I don't have time right now. Someone stabbed my cousin, and I've got to get T so we can go to the hospital," he explained, trying to walk around him, but Dez still stood in his way. "Man, what gives?"

"I've got to show you something before you leave."

Jamal shook his head. "Later with all that. I've got to get to my cousin."

He got past him and jogged up the stairs, leaving Dez regretting not finishing the job. He just hoped Chill would not make it so he could finally get Jamal's attention and they could return to how they were.

Jamal barged into the house, walking past the living room where Di'Vanni played with his sister and into the bedroom. Chantel jumped at the sudden intrusion, a tissue over her nose and her eyes a blood red. She had been crying.

Jamal paused. "You knew this whole time and you didn't tell me?"

Her eyes welled up with tears again. "What are you talking about?"

4

"You knew it was my cousin."

The next set of tears dropped freely, and she nodded. "Baby, I'm so sorry. I didn't want you to find out like this."

Jamal sighed and went to the closet to change his shirt. "What are you sorry for?" he asked and sighed. "Fuck that. It's late, so Di'Vanni can watch Lana while we're gone."

"Where are we going?"

Jamal sent her a look. "We've got to go to Regional. That's where they have Chill."

Chantel seemed taken aback, but Jamal had too much on his mind to notice as he asked her to grab the car keys and they left the house.

Outside, Dez still waited.

"Dez, watch the crib for me. The kids are in. We'll be right back."

Dez nodded. "Aight."

As they got into the car, Chantel still kept her eyes on him, unnerved when he grinned at her and then pointed to his phone.

She quickly turned away. "I don't see how you're friends with him. He creeps me out."

Jamal absently waved it off, his mind on more pressing issues. "Dez is harmless, T."

She didn't believe that.

Luckily, the hospital was about half an hour away, and Jamal and Chantel were at the front desk.

"Hey, excuse me," Jamal called, his hand finding Chantel's as he felt himself get anxious. "I'm Jamal James. I got a call that my cousin is here."

"Let's see..." The receptionist quickly checked her computer before nodding. "Oh, he's stable now. You both can head in. Room 112 down the hall. Make a left by the elevator and turn right. It's the first room, so you can't miss it."

"Thank you."

The door to the room was slightly ajar, and they could get a glimpse of the top naked man on the bed. He had an oxygen mask in place and then a tube running from his concealed abdomen and into a cylinder. The back of his hand was connected to an IV drip that transfused blood.

Chantel dry heaved. "Jamal, I don't think I can do this. I have to vomit."

Jamal freed her hand, watching as she ran down the hall before sighing and stepping into the room. As he got closer, he noticed that Chill was awake. A small smile was visible through the obscured plastic mask.

Jamal crouched beside him, the tension leaving his body when Chill's eyes met his. "Cuz, who did this to you?"

Chill's hand raised a bit, beckoning him to lean in. "Me..."

Chill's voice barely registered in his cousin's mind before the ECG picked up, the beeping gaining momentum as his breath suddenly seized.

Jamal sprung to his feet. "Chill? Chill!!"

Chill was unresponsive, and the machine began to slow once again.

"Doctor? Nurse? Anybody!" he yelled, suddenly pushed to the side as the nurses flooded in, leaving him frozen in place when they tore the oxygen off his face.

"He's going into cardiac arrest. We need the defibrillators. Now!" a doctor yelled.

Jamal could do nothing but watch as his cousin died in front of him.

Chapter Two

Remember me like Kobe...

Buck swallowed the lump in his throat as he scanned the crowd, his heart heavy with disbelief. He never imagined Chill's last favor would be asking him to speak at his funeral. The memories of their nights at the bar, sharing stories over drinks, felt like yesterday. Seeing his friend laid to rest so soon was something he hadn't and wasn't prepared for.

He looked around again, now noticing a few missing faces—Chantel and the kids—but pushed those thoughts aside, focusing on the task at hand. He had better things to worry about.

Taking a deep breath, Buck stepped forward, his free hand brushing off some imaginary dust on his new suit and then gripping the edge of the podium. The silence around him was profound, and for the last time, he looked at the closed casket before facing the sea of faces.

"Thank you all for coming today," Buck began, trying his best to keep his voice from wavering. "I'm honored to stand here and talk about Chill. We shared a lot of good times—nights at the bar, laughs over drinks, and moments that only friends who've been through it all can understand. Chill was more than a friend; he was family to me."

Buck paused, glancing down at the letter in his hand. It shook with the slightest tremble.

"Chill had a way of cutting through all the noise and speaking straight from his heart and mind, and he gave me this a while ago"—he raised the sealed letter—"and made me promise to only open it when he was gone... Hell, I thought he was just on his usual bullshit. Until now..."

He had tried so hard to keep the emotions out of his tone, but it was quickly becoming a losing battle.

He clumsily removed the stapled pins before opening the letter. With a deep breath, Buck unfolded the letter and read aloud:

"To my family and friends: 'What they talkin 'bout?' I truly love each and every one of you. It was just my time to go. I always felt like my clock was ticking. There were too many situations I couldn't escape, and I take full responsibility for them all. Maybe one day, a book will come out about me, detailing some of the wild things I've seen. That would be pretty cool.

The thing is, I never knew how to express my feelings or ask for help. I was tired out here, and you can't even begin to imagine how relieved I am now. So I don't want tears today. I want y'all to live your best lives. Let go of the petty arguments. Life's too short to wonder what people think of you. Just love everyone for who they are, what and where they are. 'Everybody won't think like you.'

Time to see my boys—Nate and Hollywood. Miss them too much to continue pretending to be happy here. The ocean was the only place I found peace, away from all the drama, where I didn't feel like a burden. My happiest moments, away from the Village.

So, let me wrap this up—My boys, make sure my ashes find the sea. Thank you all for coming. God bless, and live a wonderful life. Trust me, I'm good now, and I'm smiling. Just remember me like Kobe!

*Cedric **'Chill'** James."*

~~~

Lucky

Lucky was jolted awake by the sharp ring of his phone, and he quickly muted the call, trying his best not to disturb Nikki, who was snuggled comfortably against him. The number flashing on his screen was unfamiliar—a *336* area code.

He frowned, annoyance bubbling up. He looked at the time on the clock by the bed before groaning. It was two in the morning.

"Whoever this is calling me this late better have a damn good reason," Lucky muttered, rubbing the tiredness away from his eyes.

His movements caused Nikki to stir, her voice groggy. "Baby, who is that?"

But before Lucky could answer, a voice crackled through the phone, dripping with pure malice and venom. *"Negro, I will blow your whole shit up! You lying there with my best friend when you just had Meka pregnant with your child for the second time. Get your pathetic ass up and act like you're talking to Chill right now."*

Lucky's eyes widened for the quickest second, and for that second, he was frozen in shock. Nobody knew he was with Nikki. *Then how the hell did Chantel know?*

Nikki still watched him with slight worry before he forced a grin and leaned into her to press a quick kiss on her lips. "Babe, it's just Chill."

Feigning a calm demeanor, Lucky slipped out of bed, his gait tight. He moved quietly into the living room, hoping Nikki hadn't picked up on the tension in his voice. "What's up, my guy? I forgot your number keeps changing when you're on the water."

"Yeah, that's right. Lie like the dog you are," Chantel snarled, and he felt himself frown.

Chantel's calling always meant trouble, and the last thing he wanted to do was entertain her.

He whispered harshly into the phone. *"I'm* the dog? Like you didn't fuck Chill over and marry his cousin. Or was that someone else?"

The woman hissed on the other line, seemingly disregarding whatever retort he had to make. *"I need you to do something, and you will do it. Unless you want your secret out in the open."*

"What could you possibly want from me?" Lucky asked, his voice laced with frustration. It was way too early in the morning for this bullshit.

"The next time Chill is in town, I need to know immediately. And make sure he doesn't leave right away," Chantel demanded.

"What? You sound insane. You don't know him anymore, do you? He's not going to stick around the Village. Why the fuck would I even do anything for you?"

"I'll tell Meka you still fucking my best friend. Trust."

He felt the comeback die on his tongue before loudly exhaling. *This bitch has me by the balls.* Chantel could be extremely unpredictable, and with the path she was heading, she looked like she was looking for accomplices to drag down with her.

"What am I doing this for?" Lucky questioned after a while, resignation evident in his tone.

"None of your concern. Just make sure he sticks around, or you'll be up shit's creek without a paddle. Figure it out, dog!" Chantel hissed before hanging up.

The line went dead after that. Lucky stared at the phone, apprehension swirling in his mind and nearly giving him a headache as he fell onto the couch.

How in God's name did she expect him to pull this off?

Chapter Three

Can I live???

Chill

He had never dreamt for so long, not since he had left the Village. After what seemed like a few years of psychedelic nightmares, his eyes opened to see Jamal glaring down at him with a concerned look on his face.

"Chill, you awake?" Mal asked. "Damn, cuz, you had me scared there for a minute."

Chill tried to sit upright, watching as his cousin moved to help him before something in his back sprained. The discomfort nearly made him yell in shock and pain.

"Fuck... Why does the side of my back hurt so much?" Chill groaned.

"You've been out for at least three days," Mal explained, watching as Chill's eyes widened. Three days?! "They had to remove one of your kidneys, and you lost too much blood. It was too damaged. T and the kids would have been here, but I think she has this thing about seeing blood. It's going to take a good while for you to get back to normal."

He finally forced himself up, shaking his head stubbornly. "I need to get back to work. I need to talk to Lucky."

"Enough of all that. Work and Lucky can wait," Mal said. "What I wanna know is who's crazy enough to stab you?"

As Chill recalled the faces he'd seen that night, He remembered both of them vividly as he hesitated to answer. "I have no idea. I just remember it being dark, and my back was turned."

Mal looked at his cousin with a skeptical expression, clearly unconvinced. "For real? That ain't gonna help the police. But—"

Before Mal could ask more questions, Doctor Allen stormed in.

"I'm glad you fought to stay with us," Dr. Allen said. "Does your cousin mind if I have a word with you alone?"

Mal immediately protested. "Yeah, I mind a lot, actually. I've been here for three whole days. We've got no secrets."

As soon as Mal said that, Chill could not help but think about what had happened to Nate. No secrets, huh?

He so badly wanted to confront Jamal about it but knew it wasn't the right time. He wasn't sure there would ever be a right time to talk about something like that. Instead, he exhaled. "Mal, it's cool. It'll just be a second."

His cousin looked turn, gaze moving between him and the doctor before eventually nodding.

"Fine. I'm going to check on T and the kids and tell them you're awake," Mal said, stretching and finally leaving the room.

Once Mal was gone, Chill turned to Dr. Allen, discontent lacing the features. He could already smell his bullshit from a mile away. "How are you always around?"

The doctor smiled. "You were brought here. I work here. And I am also your doctor."

Chill narrowed his gaze. "What is it this time, Doc?"

Dr. Allen's face grew serious as he moved closer to Chill's bed, clipboard in hand. "We need to start the treatment as soon as possible. You just lost one of your kidneys. We can't be putting the other under stress by having you in poor health."

He had already thought of that as he raised an IV-infused hand to stop the doctor. "Hold off on that sermon," he interrupted. "This may sound crazy, but how's my other kidney? It's still working, right?"

Dr. Allen looked puzzled. "I'm not sure I follow."

Chill tilted a head at him like he was missing the obvious. As much as he wanted to play around the doctor's aloofness, he believed he didn't have much time.

"I'm sure you know what I'm requesting."

Dr. Allen's expression turned grave as he finally understood. "You do realize that surviving without any kidneys will require dialysis. We've already removed the other one. This will ultimately result in death."

Death...

Chill wasn't sure he wanted to die. Not yet, at least. He wasn't even sure he wanted to live. He just felt held back—like he was walking a tightrope. The stab wound that strained at every slight movement was enough to portray how he felt.

He looked away from the doctor, gaze landing on the window across from him. He felt that same gaze blur with tears.

He had made up his mind a long time ago.

15

"I'm not doing anyone any good by sticking around here, as you can see."

~~~

Jamal

Jamal pulled out his cell phone and noticed numerous missed calls and a voicemail from Dez. He decided to check the voicemail before calling Chantel.

"Mal, where are you? There's something I need to show you ASAP. Hit me back."

It sounded urgent, but he was sure he could deal with Dez later before he dialed his wife.

"Hello?" Chantel answered.

"Hey T, y'all good?"

"Yeah, we're good. What's up?"

"Chill just woke up, so you can come see him with the kids," he replied, leaning against the counter by the reception.

"Babe, can we just come later? This has been hard on all of us. Di' is still blaming himself for wanting to go to that game," Chantel explained.

"Blaming himself? Well, I'll be here until you get here..." He was about to end the call before Dez's message came to mind. "Oh! And Dez has been blowing up my phone, so I might tell him to catch a ride with you here. He supposedly has something for me to see."

There was a sigh in the background.

"I told you, Mal, there's something about him that makes me uncomfortable."

He rolled his eyes. Why did she have to be so aggravating?

"Like I keep saying, T, he's nothing to worry about. Love you!" he said, already moving to dismiss their conversation.

Chantel chewed on her bottom lip. She knew if it were Chill, he would never do anything to make her uncomfortable.

"Okay. Love you too. Bye!"

Chapter Four

Everybody is suspect...

Lucky

A news report blared from the TV as Lucky sat in front of it, eyes glued to the reporter.

"Three days and there are still no suspects in the fatal stabbing of Cedric James that occurred Friday night in a hotel parking lot. If you have any information, please contact the local police."

"Shit..." he muttered just as Nikki walked into the living room, her gaze traveling to the screen as well.

"I know that's not your friend Chill on the news," she said, her voice tinged with worry.

"I don't know for sure," Lucky replied, concerned as well. He knew damn well that was Chill's full name but could not come to terms with him. He hadn't been able to contact the man or any of his friends. "I haven't heard from him since court. I keep calling, but he's not picking up."

Nikki looked at him for a while longer before joining him on the couch, head on his legs. And just as she settled in with him, his phone rang, forcing him to reach for it. The caller ID 'Lo' relieved him.

"*Yo, why would someone kill Chill?*" Lo demanded, sounding furious and frantic. It seemed like he was walking as his breath came out in short pants.

"Wait, what? Chill is dead?!" Lucky explained as he sprang up from the seat, startling Nikki, who now looked at him with wide eyes.

"What?!" she mouthed.

"*Dude, I don't know, but I'm heading to Regional now to find out more. Buck is already on his way,*" Lo said, and Lucky was already on his seat, shrugging on some clothes.

"Come by the crib and pick me up on your way," he instructed.

"*Aight,*" And the line went dead.

Lucky roughly forced his phone into his pocket, frustration evident as he returned to the living room. *This cannot be happening.* He looked toward Nikki, who now looked equally concerned.

"Does this have anything to do with that phone call last night?"

Lucky frowned. "My friend just died, and this is what you decided to ask? Really, Nikki?"

She looked crestfallen, turning away and crossing her arms over her chest. "I don't have a good feeling about this."

Lucky didn't need to stay around to listen to her anymore as he chose to storm out of the house.

~~~

Chantel

Chantel was heading downstairs with the kids when she spotted Mal's friend Dez leaning against her car, a cigarette hanging from his lips as he frowned blankly. She always hated the man, even more now that he was sharing the car with them.

As soon as Dez saw the children, he threw his cigarette to the floor and stomped on it, a cunning smirk stretching his lips. "What's up, James family! Hi, Alani!" He crouched to give the younger daughter a high-five.

"Hey, daddy's friend!"

Dez grinned. "Such a smart kid."

"Don't speak to my child like that," Chantel snapped, pulling Alani away from him. "Di', put your sister in her car seat."

She tried to keep her tone leveled as both the kids entered the car.

As soon as the door was shut, she threw Dez a glare. "Why can't you find your own transportation?"

As she walked past him, he grabbed her arm with a firm, unsettling grip.

"I need to show you something."

She tried to twist out of his grasp but to no avail.

"I swear, if you don't let go of my arm, it'll be over for you." Her voice was low and furious, while Dez just smirked before pulling out his phone.

He immediately played a video, turning the screen to her, and Chantel's face paled when she realized what it was.

The static would make it difficult for a stranger to recognize who the two people in the video were but she knew in a heartbeat—it was her and Chill, lips locked together as they kissed in his truck before the camera abruptly panned away.

As she reached for the phone, mind frozen with shock, Dez pulled away and let her go.

"Look, *Telly*," he said with a mocking smirk, "I'm giving you 24 hours to confess. Tell Mal I'll catch up with him later."

He walked away after that, laughing to himself before lighting another cigarette, and as soon as he was gone, Chantel rid herself of the shock and hurried to the car. She strapped on her seatbelt, her mind still racing with a million panicked thoughts. *How did he know? How did he even see us? Is he going to show the video to Jamal?*

She didn't know much about Dez but could already tell he didn't bluff. He was a dangerous person alright, but the last thing she wanted to do was confess to Jamal that she had anything to do with Chill. *That would be suicide.*

"Momma, are you okay? Why do you look so worried?" Di'Vanni asked, and she whipped her head up, meeting his eyes in the rearview mirror. He had been watching her for a while.

"Yeah, baby. I'm okay," Chantel said, trying to calm her racing heart.

She soon started the car, the engine kicking to life as a final thought crossed her mind.

Dez had called her *Telly*.

And only Rashad called her by that name.

~~~

21

Chill

Jamal had talked more with Chill than he had done in years as they caught up. Chill couldn't help but wonder if it was the nerves that made his cousin talk so much, but still, he entertained the discussions. It was the most he could do when the guy had slept on the hospital couch for three nights straight.

"What was it like when you were in a coma?" Jamal asked after a while, a thoughtful expression on his face.

Chill mulled over it for a moment, exhaling. "It was just dark and peaceful."

"Peaceful?" Mal echoed, surprised.

He nodded.

It was so peaceful that he almost did not want to wake up, but before he could voice his very grim thoughts, the door swung open, revealing the woman he was sure he had seen in his many dreams.

Unique's face flushed with anger and exertion as they pouted. "I knew you better had a damn good reason for standing me up on Saturday night, and I had to hear about it on the news."

Mal looked at her with confusion. "Sorry, who are you?"

"Cedric knows who I am..." Unique replied, her gaze narrowing at Chill.

He was doing a great job at pissing off everyone, even when he did nothing.

"Cuz, this is Unique. Unique, this is my cousin, Jamal," Chill finally introduced them to each other, leaning back against his pillow. He was already itching to take a walk or jog—*anything to leave this room.*

Mal furrowed his brow. "Unique? That name sounds familiar. Do you know someone named Dezmond?"

Unique's face darkened. "Don't bring that name up in my presence. He's a deadbeat!"

Chill looked at Jamal, raising a brow. "Who is Dezmond? Mal, you know him?"

"Yeah, that's my boy. He should be on his way here with T and the kids. Let me go outside and wait for them." He was already up, apparently eager to give the two some privacy.

Chill turned back to Unique after Jamal was gone with the faintest smile. "I'm glad you came to visit."

Unique's expression softened slightly. "I just stopped by to see if it was true. I told you I don't do drama, and you look like you have some shit with you."

He felt his smile falter. "Damn, it's like that?"

She slowly nodded. "Yeah... Look, Cedric, I have a son to worry about. I can't have him experience all of... *this.* I hope you have a full recovery."

She ended with a tender kiss on his cheek before patting his shoulder. "And take care of yourself."

Chill watched her go, feeling something akin to disappointment and hurt.

Eventually, he sighed in relief. "At least that went well."

Chapter Five

Demons destroy peace...

Shay

The news about the stabbing had been everywhere, and Shay couldn't shake the image of CJ lying in that parking lot. The guilt gnawed at her, keeping her from sleep. She still couldn't believe she had actually stabbed him. CJ had been good to her, but the lies—oh, the lies—had been too much to bear.

Her mother walked into the bedroom, interrupting her thoughts.

"Hey, Ma," Shay greeted, trying to sound normal.

"Baby, you've been cooped up in this house for three days now. What's going on?" her mother asked, her tone soft but probing.

"Nothing. Just tired," Shay replied, forcing a smile that didn't reach her eyes.

"You hear about that stabbing in the Holiday Inn parking lot? It's been all over the news," her mother continued, oblivious to Shay's inner turmoil.

"No, I haven't been watching any TV," Shay lied, her stomach tightening. The last thing she wanted her mother to know was that she had connections with Chill.

"I think his name was Cedric..." Her mother had a thoughtful expression for a moment before snapping her fingers. "You two are around the same age. Hold up... I remember him now. Baby, isn't that the boy you went to college with? From the Ville or something? Didn't he live with us for a while?"

Shay's heart stuttered, and she felt it leap to her throat. "Yes, ma'am, that's him. He's always been on the water," she said, her voice barely above a whisper.

Her mother sighed, a wistful smile on her face. "Aren't you a little concerned for your friend? I loved him. He was such a nice young man, always seemed troubled by something. I just wanted to hug him and never let go."

Shay tried to keep her composure, her leg crossing over the other in discomfort. "He was just... okay," she replied, but her voice betrayed her.

"Okay? Shute, girl, in my day, I'd be right up under him—or on top, making a baby," her mother joked, trying to lighten the mood.

"Momma, you're crazy!" Shay said, forcing a laugh.

"Whatever! I just heard he woke up. Praise God! He was in a coma for the last couple of days. You should go visit him. You two were real close."

Under her breath, Shay muttered, "Oh shit..."

~~~

Lucky

Lo pulled into the hospital parking garage and immediately spotted Buck leaning against a car, his phone out as he flirted with a nurse who had just finished her shift. Lo and Lucky exchanged a knowing look as they exited the car, laughing.

"Buck, what's up?" Lo called out.

"Man, I see you," Lucky added, smirking.

Buck grinned, unbothered. "Saw her from across the lot. I was just trying to get some information on Chill."

"Yeah, right. Her number definitely has a lot of information on him," Lucky quipped.

Buck chuckled. "Chill would understand."

Lucky's expression turned serious as he recalled the exact reason they were at the hospital. "Buck, when's the last time you talked to Chill?"

Buck's smile faded. "We had a couple of drinks, then he remembered he had court. Somebody flattened his tires that day."

"What? Who?" Lucky asked, frowning.

Buck shrugged. "You know Chill, ain't no telling. He said he was calling Chantel to pick him up."

Lo shook his head. "He needs to let that go."

"That's what I told him," Buck replied as they all turned to see a familiar face approaching—Unique.

Lucky leaned in and whispered to Lo and Buck, "Matter of fact, I left Chill talking to her at court."

"Hey, fellas," Unique greeted them with a casual wave. "I just talked to your boy."

"Chill?" Lo asked.

"Who else would I be talking about?" Unique replied, rolling her eyes.

"He's alive?" Lucky asked, his voice tinged with hope.

"He sure seemed that way before I left," Unique said, her tone indifferent.

"What did he say?" Buck asked, his curiosity piqued.

Unique sighed. "Nothing worth mentioning. I just wanted to see if he was okay."

She started to walk away, but Lucky called after her. He felt like she had cut ties with Chill but had an odd obligation to help his friend out at least. "You know he always had a thing for you."

Unique paused for a moment but kept walking, her face set in a determined expression. Yeah, he's lost her.

"Let's go. Hold on... Is that Chantel?" Lo asked, spotting a SUV pulling into a parking space with her kids in the backseat.

Chantel stepped out of the car, a broad smile on her face when she spotted Buck and Lo. "Oh my God! Hey, Mont... I haven't seen you in years. Hey, Kalo!" she said, rushing over to hug them.

She completely ignored Lucky, who stood right next to them. His expression darkened.

"You forgetting someone?" Lucky asked, his voice laced with bitterness.

Chantel didn't even glance his way. "Nope. Come on, kids, let's go see your Uncle C!" she called out, ushering her children toward the hospital.

This bitch...

"You are something else," Lucky muttered under his breath, shaking his head.

Lo called after her. "Chantel, do you know anything about Chill's current condition?"

Chantel paused, her earlier cheerfulness fading as she shook her head. "No. My husband just called me and said he finally woke up."

Lucky's lip curled into a bitter smirk. "Your husband Mal... He's Chill's cousin, right? First cousin?"

Chantel shot him a sharp look. "You care to share your secret? I'm not in the mood right now."

As they all began walking toward the hospital, Di'Vanni held onto his sister, but Alani broke free, sprinting toward the entrance.

"Hey, Daddy! I missed you!" Alani called, beaming as she ran toward Jamal, who leaned against a pillar.

Mal greeted them, scooping Alani up into his arms. "T, what took y'all so long? And what's up, guys? I guess the word got around fast."

"How is he?" Lo asked, concerned.

Mal smiled faintly. "You know how Chill is."

Lucky exhaled in relief. "That bastard... He sure is stubborn."

Mal's smile widened. "You know it," he said. "Only three people can be in the room right now."

"We'll let the kids go in first," Lo suggested.

Mal turned to Chantel. "T, I thought Dez was supposed to catch a ride with you?"

Chantel hesitated. "He said he would catch up with you later."

Jamal's smile faltered for a second. "Right... You and the kids can go in first. The doctor says it would be good for him to see some different faces."

Chapter Six

Life is short...

Chill

As Chantel and the kids walked into the hospital room, Chill immediately sat up, his heart racing. The last time he saw all of them was when Chantel delivered news that changed everything. The kids ignored the IV tubes crisscrossing his half-naked body as they rushed to hug him.

"Hey, family!" Chill greeted, his smile not being forced for once as he kissed Alani's forehead. "You two been good to your mom? Di, I'm sorry I missed the game."

Di'Vanni's voice quivered with guilt. "It's my fault you got stabbed."

Chill shook his head firmly. "How is that even possible? Di, people are crazy. Don't ever think you had something to do with this. I'll be back to my old self in no time."

Chantel, still shaken, asked, "Do you know who did this to you?" with worry etched on her face.

Chill looked away for a second before shaking his head. "It was dark, and my back was turned. Didn't see a thing."

There was a bit of silence as Alani traced over his stomach before pausing. "Mommy, why does Uncle Chill have your name 'T-E-L—"

"Chantel, I've got to tell you something. It's important."

Chantel leaned in closer, keen to hear what he had to say. "What... What's up?"

"I lost my kidney," Chill whispered back, his voice strained. "I've got just—"

Chantel's eyes widened, but before she could respond or he could finish, Jamal's voice boomed from the doorway, cutting through the tension. "You two got a secret I need to know about?"

Chill quickly recovered, sitting up and taking Alani with him with a forced smile. "Of course not. Just asking your wife how you're holding up."

His cousin snorted. "Me? Look at you. You should hire security at this point. A couple of your homies are here to see you. I'll send them up. Kids, let's give Uncle C a couple of minutes."

As they all left the room, heading towards the lobby, Chill could not help but notice the odd look in Jamal's eyes as he stared at Chantel. He wondered how long Jamal had been standing by the doorway and how much he had heard.

Chill's face lit up as his friends rushed in, greeting him with their signature handshakes.

Lo grinned but couldn't hide his concern. "Man, what the hell you got going on?"

Chill tried to play it off. "What do you mean? I don't have beef with anyone."

Buck leaned in, his tone serious, while Lo took a seat beside the bed. "You do remember you stay hot around here, right?"

Lucky crossed his arms, staring at Chill. "Do you know who did it?"

31

Chill shook his head slightly. "Not really, but I need one of you to find my phone."

Lucky raised an eyebrow. "I've been hitting your line."

"Yeah, I don't know where it is," Chill admitted. "I need to holla at Sizzle."

"Sizzle?" Lucky's gaze seemed distant for a moment as Chill raised a brow at him.

"You got your phone on you? I need to call her real quick. You still have her number, right?"

Lucky nodded, but his hesitation was noticeable. "I do, but I left my phone in Lo's car."

Lo frowned before standing. "No problem, I'll go get it."

"Nah, it's probably dead. You know I stay with 10% battery life," Lucky replied, stopping him with a small chuckle.

Buck rolled his eyes, his hand going into his pocket. "Here, just use mine."

Chill dialed Shay's number, but it kept ringing without an answer. The tension in the room thickened, and Lucky's gaze stayed on Chill, who, for the life of him, did not know why. Did he know something he didn't?

"Damn, no answer," Chill muttered after a third try, handing the phone back to Buck.

He smiled, insistent on lightening the mood. "Fellas, I'm glad you stopped by, but I'm needing my meds and a sponge bath from one of these fine nurses. Tell everyone else I'm good, and I'll be out of here soon. Love y'all, boys!"

As they exited the room, Chill could not help but watch Lucky.

He was sure he had seen him with a phone when he first entered the hospital room.

Chapter Seven

Trust God

Dr. Allen

Dr. Allen entered the room, greeted by the sight of the entire family gathered around Cedric "Chill" James. He had seen his fair share of family drama over the years, but this felt like a scene straight out of a lifetime movie. He fumbled slightly with his chart before speaking, trying to prepare for the potential storm brewing.

"Alright," Dr. Allen began, clearing his throat, "Looks like you'll be able to get out of here soon. But we've got a long road of recovery ahead."

Chill cut in, his frustration barely contained. "When can I get out of this dump and back to work?"

Dr. Allen raised an eyebrow, already sensing the pushback. "Work? You lost a kidney, Cedric. A full recovery will take 6 to 12 weeks, and that includes physical therapy."

Chill clenched his jaw, irritation bubbling under the surface. He wanted to lash out so badly, but he kept quiet for the kids' sake.

Mal, sensing the tension, stepped in. "Doc, what do you need from us to make sure he gets healthy?"

Dr. Allen glanced at Chill, then back to Mal. "He's going to need at-home care."

Chill scoffed. "I don't live around here, Doc. You've been my doctor for years and still don't know that?"

Mal waved it off. "It's okay. You're staying with us."

Chantel quickly interjected, her tone laced with concern. "Babe, I don't think that's a good idea."

Chill was quick to agree.

"Matter of fact, it's a terrible idea."

Dr. Allen looked between them, his concern growing. "Is this going to be a problem?"

Jamal threw up his hands in exasperation. "Then where the fuck would you stay?" he asked Chill. "I've got you covered, cuz. I'm just not wiping your butt."

His cousin could be funny as hell when he wanted to be.

Chill forced a smirk. "Funny guy. My hands aren't broken."

Chantel added, trying to sound reasonable. "Our apartment is upstairs. It can be rough going up and down, and we only have a two-bedroom."

Jamal waved her off, attempting to brush off her concerns. "I'll help him up the steps. He'll be alright once he gets up there. Our couch pulls out into a bed. Chill, this is one of the first times I don't see that grin on your face. All you're doing is sleeping and taking meds. Too easy!"

Alani chimed in with innocent enthusiasm. "Yeah, I like it when Uncle C stays around."

He grinned at his daughter.

"See? My baby knows it's a good idea."

Chill and Chantel exchanged a look of concern.

They both knew nothing good would come from this arrangement. Di'Vanni, despite being quiet, was observing everything, his young eyes sharp.

Dr. Allen, sensing unresolved tension, cleared his throat. "Well, now that that's settled, we can discuss the other issue."

Jamal's eyes narrowed. "What other issue?"

Chill cut in sharply, shutting it down. "There is no other issue. Thanks, Doc, for your perfect timing. You've been great."

Dr. Allen, visibly frustrated but unwilling to push further, stood up and exhaled. "I think you all should go and make accommodations for Cedric. I'll have him ready to go in a couple of hours. Cedric, I wish this were under different circumstances."

Chill stared right through Dr. Allen as he left the room, fuming at how close the doctor had come to spilling his secrets.

Jamal nudged him, sensing his foul mood. "Don't worry, cuz. We'll make you feel at home."

~~~

Shay

She woke up from a nap and noticed a missed call from an unfamiliar number. The area code was the same as Chill's. Could Chill have been trying to reach her? She had taken his phone when he was bleeding out and had been trying to break into it ever since. Curiosity gnawing at her, Shay decided to call the unknown number back.

"Hello?" Buck's voice answered on the other end.

"Did someone try calling this number earlier?" Shay asked, trying to keep her voice steady.

"Oh shit, yeah!" Buck replied, his tone surprised. "I'm Buck. Is your name Sizzle? Chill was trying to contact you."

"No, my name is Shay. What did he want with me?" She gulped as she waited for a response.

"He and Lucky were talking, and he just mentioned your name. It seemed important. He lost his phone the night he was stabbed. I can give you his room number so you can be transferred in case you wanna talk to him."

Shay hesitated, feeling the weight of the situation. "Okay."

"Room 112. He must really like you," Buck added, his tone teasing.

Shay narrowed her eyes at the sudden change of topic. "Why do you say that?"

"I've heard him mention your name before. He hardly talks about anyone twice.

"Thanks," Shay said curtly, dismissing the topic. The last thing she wanted to do was begin to feel guilty, but she could not help the relief that swept through her as she realized he was not dead. "Nice meeting you, Buck. Bye."

As she hung up, Shay debated whether to call Chill back. After a lot of pondering, she searched for the hospital number.

~~~

37

Chill

Roc and MJ had come to visit as well and were more than relieved when Chill said he was going to be discharged. Chill appreciated them coming. He appreciated that almost the entire neighborhood cared enough to see how he was doing.

As Roc stood up to leave, the hospital landline began to ring, and he handed the phone to Chill. "I think it's for you."

"Aight, y'all boys be safe. Thanks for coming!" Chill said, watching them head out.

MJ shot back, "Nah, you be safe. You're the one in the hospital."

It seemed to be everyone's favorite line at that moment.

As they left, Chill put the phone to his ear. "Hello?"

"What do you want, CJ?" her voice was cold, almost detached.

Chill felt his mouth hang open as he heard her voice. He could recognize it anywhere. Shay had the prettiest feathery voice. "You hate me so much that you'd leave me for dead?"

"What do you want, CJ?" She must have tried to sound nonchalant, but he could hear the waver in her tone.

"I know you have my phone, Sizzle," he said flatly.

"There's nothing of yours I have," she shot back.

He sighed and leaned into the pillows Alani had diligently fluffed for him. "Cut the act already. I could have told the police everything by now."

"So why didn't you?" she challenged, the fear in her voice was more palpable now.

38

"Because I love you more than you realize?"

Shay scoffed. *"Don't feed me that bullshit."*

Chill could feel a headache brewing. It would be difficult to explain anything to the woman, especially after what she had done, but still, he chose to try.

"I'm being serious, Shay. You know I tried to keep you out of my drama. My life is too messy for you. Hell, I don't even know what I did to make you so mad."

Shay's laugh was bitter. *"Negro, you had me drop you off at the airport just for you to turn around and hop in the car with someone else."*

Chill's brow furrowed. *Someone else?*

He exhaled, not wanting to continue the argument.

"Just... answer the phone whenever I call, okay? I'll explain when I'm out. And I forgive you, okay?" Life was too short to hold petty grudges, and he had experienced it first-hand.

He moved to end the call before Shay blurted out. *"Wait, CJ!"*

"What?" he asked.

"Who was that girl who called me to tell me you were still in town?"

Chill's brows furrowed. "Huh?"

"That's how I knew you were still in town," Shay continued, her voice trembling slightly. *"Some girl called me after I dropped you off."*

Chill suddenly sat up. "What? Do you still have the number?"

"It was from an unknown number," Shay admitted. *"She was laughing about you lying about leaving. She called right after I dropped you off."*

Chill's mind raced as he absently ended the call.

At first, he had overlooked the various signs, but now, it was clear as day—somebody wanted to take him out. And from the look of things, he couldn't help but feel he already knew the person.

Chapter Eight

A lie or a secret?

The tension was palpable as Chantel and Mal pulled up to their apartment complex, Chill laid out in the backseat like a ticking time bomb. Every time he set foot in this place, something bad happened. It was either Jamal and Chantel argued, or he found out his nephew was actually his son. As they all stepped out of the car, their eyes fixed on the first step, Chill could not help but feel uneasy.

He turned to his cousin. "Mal, I don't know about these steps."

Jamal tried to reassure him as he leaned against the car with his crutches. "It'll be fine. I'll even get my boy Dez to help!"

"Dez?" Chill echoed, his suspicion growing. He had heard the name too many times.

"You know my boy Dez," Mal said, lighting a cigarette as if it was the most natural thing in the world. "Lives here as well."

Chill shook his head. "Nah, I don't think we ever formally met."

Sensing the growing tension, Chantel stepped in. "I'm about to get the kids settled upstairs."

Mal held up a hand, stopping her. "Wait a second, T. I'll go get Dez."

He was already around the corner as Chantel turned to Di'Vanni. "Di', take your sister upstairs. We'll be right up in a minute."

Di'Vanni hesitated, sensing something was off. "Mommy, you sure?"

Chill, trying to mask his growing dread, forced a smile. "Di', we're good here."

The boy nodded reluctantly. "Okay. Uncle C, be careful."

"I will," he reassured.

Chantel watched as her kids disappeared up the steps, the uneasy feeling growing in her gut. "I don't like this."

Chill echoed her concern. "Who is this dude I keep hearing about?"

Before Chantel could respond, he and Dez appeared, talking and laughing as they walked up, both puffing on cigarettes. The moment Dez spoke, Chill froze. He recognized that voice before he could see who owned it. *That sneer.* His blood ran cold.

He glared in shock, whispering to himself. "You've got to be kidding me."

Chantel looked at him, alarmed. "What's wrong?"

Chill's eyes were locked on Dez, his mind racing. "I know him—and that fucking frown—from anywhere. He was there the night I was stabbed."

Chantel's eyes widened in shock. "Cedric, are you sure?"

"Positive," Chill said, his voice low and dangerous. He cursed himself for not having a weapon on him. "He also pulled a gun on me. He was driving a black BMW, smoking a cigarette."

Mal approached, oblivious to the storm brewing between them. "Hey, T, you can head up now. We got this."

Chantel glanced at Chill, her eyes brimming with fear, before she looked back at Dez. He was standing there, tapping his watch with a smirk that always sent a shiver down her spine.

Chill's voice cut through the air, cold and sharp. "Nobody touch me. Don't I know you from somewhere?"

Dez's smirk deepened as he took a step forward. "You ain't in no shape to be questioning me."

Mal's eyes darted between them, the realization slowly dawning on him. "Do you two know each other?"

Chill's eyes never left Dez's face. "Cuz, I don't need this ugly fucker helping me. He pulled a gun on me the day I was stabbed."

Mal's disbelief morphed into anger. "What?"

Dez quickly pulled out his phone. "Mal, this dude is a snake. He's been kissing your—"

But before he could finish, Mal's fist collided with Dez's face, sending him crashing to the ground. His phone shattered as it hit the pavement, the screen splintering across the concrete.

Jamal stood over Dez, his glare dark with anger. Dez wiped the blood from his lip, his eyes dark with anger and something more—betrayal. "You're gonna regret that, Mal."

Chill couldn't help but watch as a black BMW—eerily similar to the one that had attacked him—pulled up, roughly hitting the brakes inches away from Chill.

As Dez staggered to his feet, glaring at them both, Chantel stepped closer to Chill, her heart pounding.

"Touch my brother one more time—" A voice intervened, Rashad, jogging to them. Jamal immediately shoved him away, but he retaliated by throwing a punch in his direction.

"Rashad!"

Rashad turned to Chantel with a glare before moving to help his brother up. "Bro, grab your phone and get in the fucking car. Telly, you're fired!"

There was a lot of hesitance on Dez's part, but Rashad pulled him away.

"Mal, you picking this bastard over me?" he yelled at Jamal. "I thought we had love for each other!"

Jamal was fuming as Rashad led Dez away while Chantel stared in disbelief. Chill could not help but ponder. *Love?*

Chapter Nine

Juice not worth the squeeze...

Rashad

The car's engine roared as Dez and Rashad sped down the darkened streets, leaving behind the chaos of the fight. Rashad's grip on the wheel tightened, his eyes narrowing to slits as a younger version of Chill's face surged into his mind. He knew the man from somewhere but could not pinpoint where. Rashad rarely forgot a face, especially one that he had a history with.

"Man, what the fuck was that about?" His voice broke the silence, thick with irritation. His knuckles whitened as he took a sharp turn, barely checking his rearview mirror. He could sense his younger brother's eyes widen. "Just came down to check on you 'cause you've been ignoring my calls, and I see you getting your ass beat. What's up with that?"

Dez, slouched in the passenger seat, rubbed his sore nose. "It's nothing, bro. Just a disagreement—fuck, I think he broke my nose." He looked at the shattered device in his hand. "And now my phone's busted."

Rashad scoffed, his patience wearing thin. "Fuck that phone. Now you got me wrapped up in some shit. Who were those clowns?"

Dez exhaled slowly, a sense of dread creeping in. "You know who Jamal is. Telly's old man... and his cousin, Chill."

"Chill?" Rashad's brow furrowed, recognition budding at the back of his head. "I think I know that name... Does he go by anything else?"

Dez shifted uncomfortably. "Cedric or CJ, I think..."

Rashad's eyes darkened, the pieces finally clicking. *Of fucking course.* It had been over a decade, but the man still had to come back and haunt him.

"CJ," he muttered, the tone laced with malice. "The bastard at the store back then... Jamal went to prison because of him, yeah?"

He remembered the cocky expression on Chill's face, and after so many years, it still hadn't changed. And now, Jamal was defending him. *Again.* Rashad knew he had to do something about it.

Dez nodded, slowly gulping. "Yeah, that's him."

Rashad's jaw ticked as he turned into the hospital parking lot. "Hell yeah. I never forget a face. And trust me, they've got what's coming." His brother watched him from the corner of his eye, hesitation creeping into his gaze. "What?"

Dez sighed. "I don't know, man... Can you not get Mal tied up in this?"

His brow raised in surprise and mild annoyance.

"The fuck? He literally broke your nose," he said as he parked the car and turned off the engine. "Come on. Let's get it checked."

Dez reluctantly got out of the car as well. "I'm the one that has a problem with him. Just take care of Chill if you can."

~~~

46

Chill

Back at the apartment, Chill sat stiffly on the pull-out couch, grimacing as he shifted to find a comfortable position. The faint sound of Mal slamming his bedroom door echoed down the hall. Chill eventually leaned against a propped-up pillow, redirecting his gaze to the ceiling, his mind racing. Something was off.

Jamal stormed into the living room, rubbing his nose and muttering.

"You good?" Chill asked, his voice calm but probing. "You look like you're catching a cold or something. I mean, if you don't want me here, I can make other arrangements."

His cousin immediately shook his head, still pacing. "It's not that," he muttered, wiping his nose again. "Dez... he's like family, you know? I told him not to mess with you, but now..."

Chill's brow furrowed. "Dez? What's the deal with him?"

Mal let out a bitter laugh, his eyes clouded with guilt. "Can you believe his brother's the one from the *Fast Lane* store all those years back?"

Chill paused, finally able to pinpoint where he had seen that face before. "Fuck... You think he knows?"

Mal dropped into a chair, running his hands over his face. "I don't know, man. Everything's so messed up."

The room fell into an uncomfortable silence, both men lost in their thoughts. Finally, Chill spoke, his voice low and measured. "Look, I'm not trying to come between you two. I know how tight bonds like that can be. You remember how Nate and I were?"

Jamal froze, suddenly finding the fabric on the couch more interesting than their conversation.

He finally cleared his throat, forcing a smile as he looked back at Chill. "Yeah, I remember. Like you and me."

Chill nodded, raising his fist to bump Jamal. "Yeah... Family over everything, right?"

Jamal returned the bump, but something in his expression did not sit right with Chill. "Right."

He studied his cousin quietly, noticing the slight tremor in Mal's hands, the sniffing, the restless energy.

"Mal," he started slowly, "how long have you been using?"

Jamal's eyes snapped up. "Using what?"

Chill sighed, leaning back. "You know what I'm talking about. I've seen the signs. You doing that mess around the kids?"

Mal bristled, defensiveness creeping into his tone. "Don't worry about what I do in my own house, and besides, it's just to take the edge off. It's not like I'm hooked on it or anything."

Chill didn't buy it.

He knew and had heard a lot about Jamal's substance problem. What he could see was his cousin having a withdrawal. *Either that or something pretty big is bugging him.*

"I've heard that stuff makes people do crazy things. Makes them angry too. You sure you're good?"

His cousin gave the stiffest nod before looking away.

"I think you've got enough on your plate without worrying about me. I'm good, alright?"

~~~

Nikki

Across town, Nikki sat on her couch, biting her lip as she stared at her phone. Lucky had been gone all day, and his phone kept going straight to voicemail. The pit in her stomach grew as the news broadcast replayed in her head, the story about the stabbing flashing across her eyes again and again.

Unable to shake off the anxiety she felt, she called Chantel.

Chantel picked up after the first ring, her voice tense. *"Please tell me you've got good news. It's been a fucking shitstorm today."*

"Good news?" Nikki sighed. "I'm so sorry to hear about Cedric. I can't believe all this is happening."

Chantel hissed. *"Cedric will be fine. He's staying with us for now. Besides, I got fired today. That's more important."*

Nikki frowned. "Damn, girl, don't you care about Chill at all?"

Chantel's voice was dismissive. *"He'll manage. This wasn't even my idea. He's only here because Mal insisted."*

Nikki chuckled, sensing the drama brewing. The two used to be obsessed with each other before Jamal came into the picture, and now, it was a completely different story. "I swear, I need popcorn for this. You two can't stand each other."

"It's a nightmare. You know we can't be around each other for long. And now, with everything happening with Di'Vanni..."

Nikki's tone softened. "You haven't told him about Di'Vanni yet, have you?"

There was a bit of reluctance on the other line.

"I... had to. My baby's getting sicker every day, and on top of it all, Chill had to get stabbed and lose the one thing we needed."

Nikki swallowed thickly, her throat tight with shock and guilt. She wasn't sure she could hide it any longer. "Who would do something like that?" she managed a whisper.

Chantel's voice turned icy. *"I don't know. All he's told me is that he lost his phone. He's not saying anything else."*

Nikki sighed, her guilt bubbling to the surface. "Look, girl, there's something I need to tell you. And I don't feel good about it..."

"God... what did you do?"

Chapter Ten

Family ties...

Jamal

Mal stepped out into the cool night air, his mind spinning from everything that had happened. He was high as a kite but was still unable to brush off the uneasiness of everything he felt, with Chill dropping Nate in the middle of their conversation. He had gone so long without thinking about the guy, and now, he was everywhere.

Jamal was sorry to an extent.

It was supposed to be Chill, not Nate, but at this moment, he could not fathom losing his cousin, who was the only family member he had left. *And Dez...*

He fumbled for his phone, trying Dez's number again. He needed answers to a lot of things, and somehow, he could feel Dez could help clear things up even though he had pointed a gun at his cousin.

For the third time, the call went straight to voicemail, and he groaned.

"Come on, Dez..." Mal muttered, clenching his jaw. "Call me back when you get this. We need to talk, man. I need your side of the story. This shit ain't adding up."

He hung up, stuffing the phone into his pocket as he walked through the quiet streets with no exact destination in mind. His head was just too clouded.

~~~

Chantel

Chantel emerged from her bedroom, her heart thudding in her chest. She spotted Chill sprawled out on the couch, asleep, his face etched with exhaustion. For a moment, she hesitated, watching him, a yearning in her chest so strong it hurt. She wanted to be close to him—closer than she ever could be now. A part of her wished she could just crawl into his skin, make everything between them whole again.

Suddenly, Chill jerked awake, his body stiffening as if sensing her presence.

"You can't stay here..." she said, forcing a frown on her lips.

He blinked, sitting up with a groan. "No shit, Tel. You think I wanna be here? What the hell do you think this feels like for me?"

Chantel crossed her arms, biting her lip. "Why are you protecting the person who stabbed you?"

Chill rubbed his temple, undoubtedly feeling his head ache and then exhaling slowly. "I'm not protecting anyone. But there's something bigger going on, something we need to handle first."

Chantel's face paled. *He just has to bring it up.* But she couldn't deny that it was a more pressing issue.

Her voice lowered as she glanced toward the hallway where her children were. "I'm scared for Di'Vanni, Cedric."

Chill's gaze softened. "I'll figure it out, Tel. Just be ready. You'll know when it's time."

She didn't understand what he meant but nodded, completely trusting him as it came naturally to her. Things used to be so easy then. Where did it all go wrong?

There was a pause, the weight of unsaid things hanging in the air between them. Chill finally looked at her again. "Come on, what's up with you?"

Chantel felt her eyes blur with tears.

"That was Alani's father back there," she said in a whisper, watching as his eyes widened into a furious glare.

"What the fuck? Of all fucking people. Your boss? The same dude me and Mal got into it with before I even met you?"

"How was I supposed to know?" Chantel whispered back fiercely. "You and Mal keep so many damn secrets. How could I have known?"

Chill shook his head, a bitter smile tugging at his lips. "Small world, ain't it?"

She hummed in agreement, discreetly wiping her eyes as memories of their past flooded back. She wanted to go back to them so badly. "Cedric... do you ever think about us?"

His smile turned sour, and he exhaled loudly. "I never stopped thinking about you. Not for a second. I'll love you till my last breath, Chantel, and you know it."

Tears welled in her eyes, but she held them back. "From the day I met you... and every time I look at our son. I've never stopped loving you."

Chill sighed, the pain of lost time weighing on him. "You could've just asked me to stay. No need to drag Lucky into it."

Chantel's breath hitched. "You knew?"

"I'm tired, Tel," Chill said, leaning back against the couch, at the same time dismissing her. "Let me rest. I need to focus on recovering."

Chantel's voice trembled as she whispered, "Are you mad at me? I'm sorry, Cedric."

"Nah," Chill said softly, his eyes half-closed. "Just disappointed. Crazy, right? This is the most we've talked since we were kids."

They both chuckled softly, the tension breaking for a brief moment. Chantel bent down, pressing her lips to his in a tender, passionate kiss. It was a kiss filled with everything unsaid, with regret, longing, and love. When she pulled away, her eyes met his with what she could recognize as fondness and regret. Her heart pounded in her chest, but before she could say anything, she saw a shadow in the doorway.

Di'Vanni stood there, watching them with a small, knowing smile. He looked at his mother before heading for the kitchen, but before he could get there, his body suddenly swayed, and he fell to the ground.

"Di'Vanni!" Chantel screamed, rushing to his side. "Oh my God! Chill, call 911!"

Chapter Eleven

No concept of time...

Chill

Chill stood outside the clinic, a cool breeze brushing against his face as he gazed at the building one last time. He'd spent weeks coming here in secret, rebuilding his strength, adjusting to life with one kidney. It was a painful process, but now, finally, he was ready. His plan was in motion, and he knew time was running out—for both him and Di'Vanni. As he rang the ceremonial bell in the therapy room, a wave of finality washed over him.

His recovery was complete, but it wasn't the kind of victory he could celebrate. This was just one step toward what had to be done.

Dr. Allen, the same man who had seen him through every painful session, approached with a clipboard in hand, offering a rare smile. "You've really surprised me, Cedric. The progress you've made—I'm shocked, really."

Chill gave a dry laugh, his eyes hollow. "I haven't been in this much pain in a long time, but you know what comes next, though, Doc. This ain't the end of the road."

Dr. Allen studied him briefly, his brow furrowed in thought and uncertainty. "You've carried all this weight on your own, without your family knowing the truth so far... Are you sure you're ready?"

He gave a dull nod, shrugging his shoulders. They were better off not knowing anyway, and his kidney would be in much better hands. "It's been a while since I've been this sure about anything."

The doctor extended a hand, his expression grim. "Take care of yourself, Mr. James, and I'll see you soon."

Chill felt his eyes sting with wetness and quickly wiped the single tear that threatened to escape before accepting the handshake. "Always, Doc. See you soon."

He kept the fake smile on his face as he left the hospital and climbed into his truck, the weight of everything bore down on him. He stared at his phone, debating, then dialed Shay from his new number.

The phone rang twice before the familiar voice answered, her tone full of suspicion. *"Who is this?"*

Chill leaned back, closing his eyes at the sound of her voice. "Hey, baby. Now lie to me and tell me you miss me."

"Boy, you're so damn crazy." Shay's laugh was light, almost playful.

He chuckled as well, their laughter echoing across the line like she had not tried to kill him not too long ago.

Chill breathed out, winding up his windows and turning on the *AC.* "How have you been, Shay?"

"You know me, CJ. I'm a survivor. Always have been."

Chill's voice softened, almost sincere. "Well, I'm gonna make sure you don't have to feel that way anymore. But I need a favor. You remember my cousin, right?"

There was a small pause on the other line.

"Yeah, I remember him."

With that, Chill laid out the details of what he needed. After the call ended, he sat in silence, looking out the window to find that it was pouring outside. The muffled downpour soothed him in a way. He sighed and opened his keypad once more to dial another number, and after the third try, the call connected.

"Yo."

"Man, I'm glad your number never changes. I'd be in trouble if it did," he replied, putting the phone on speaker and leaving it on the armrest.

Lucky chuckled. *"Ain't that the truth? How's it been living with your girlfriend? Chantel still can't stand my ass, huh?"*

"She's been cool, but that's not what I called for."

Lucky's tone shifted. *"You sound serious. What's up?"*

Chill's voice dropped, his words slow, measured. "Why didn't you just tell me about that party back in the day? About them getting married... and then you telling Nikki to call Sizzle and drag her into this? What the fuck were you thinking, bro?"

Silence.

Lucky did not answer right away, the weight of the accusation hanging in the air.

"You hurt me, man. But it wasn't the anger—it was the confusion. You really fucked up that day in the hospital. You left your phone in the car, and you never do that. I mean, *never*. I picked up on that back when we were teenagers."

Lucky sighed, his voice heavy with what Chill could only imagine to be regret. *"I know, man. I'm sorry. I got caught up in my own mess, just thinking about myself... I—Di'Vanni is your kid, right?"*

Chill's voice was cold. "Doesn't matter."

"Fuck... I had a feeling he was. Me and even the guys too."

He didn't feel like hearing any of it as he rubbed his face with his palm, feeling exhaustion creep in. "I've got a lot to take care of. You be safe out here."

"Be safe? You talk like you're going somewhere," Lucky asked.

Chill paused, the finality of his words settling in. "Yeah, I am. It's time for me to move on. This is the longest I've stayed home."

"Wait. Where are you—"

But it was too late. Chill had already hung up, looking at the number for the very last time.

He sighed to himself and started the truck engine, observing that the rain had reduced to a drizzle as he drove out of the hospital parking lot and back to the house. He was going to miss the place and everything about it. *Speaking of which—* he had one last call to make, and the person answered in a second.

"What's up, cuz?" Jamal greeted him, and he breathed a laugh.

He tapped on his steering wheel as he waited for the traffic light to change. "I've got something for you."

Mal's voice perked up. *"Oh yeah? What's that?"*

Chill gave a lopsided smirk, feeling the weight of all the secrets hanging between them. "It's just something to help you knock that edge off."

Chapter Twelve

Thomasville, North Carolina Exit 103...

The living room was filled with the familiar sounds of the family—laughter, the soft hum of a movie, and the occasional murmur from Chill, who sat quietly watching Di'Vanni nestled beside him. Everything seemed peaceful, as if they were just a normal family on a quiet night. But the peace shattered with a loud knock on the door. Chantel looked out the window and saw Dezmond standing alongside a sheriff. As always, the man had a smirk on his face as he winked and then pointed at the door.

Chantel turned to Jamal, unease setting in. "Your friend is outside... with a cop."

"Dez?" Mal asked, squinting through the window as well. "Oh, that's him."

Chill looked up from his spot on the couch across from them and then tapped Di'Vanni, who leaned against him.

"Di'... take Lani and go to your room. Grown folks have something to handle real quick."

Di'Vanni was reluctant but nodded. "Okay, but make sure you pause the movie, Uncle C," he said and got up with his sister.

As soon as they left, Jamal headed for the door and opened it.

The sheriff stepped forward before Dez, looking around before his gaze settled on Chantel. "Are you Chantel James?"

Chantel nodded, her voice hesitant. "Yes, that's me. What's this ab—"

"You've been served," the sheriff interrupted, handing her a thick envelope with no further utterance, leaving her to stare in surprise as he walked away.

Chantel ripped the envelope open, reading through the documents before her mouth fell open and the papers slipped from her grasp. She was soon outside after the sheriff, screaming at the top of her lungs.

"He can't do this. He can't take her away from me!" she yelled down the hall.

Chill didn't know whether to go after her or see the documents, but Jamal decided fast, squatting to retrieve them.

His face changed as he read through the documents, his jaw tightening, and Chill's eyes widened when he got a glance at the fine print. It had all gone to hell at that point.

"Mal, I think you need to take a breath," Chill suggested, attempting to collect the envelope, but Jamal lunged at him, hand against Chill's throat as he shoved him aside.

"And I think you need to stay out of my fucking way," Jamal growled, marching up to the bedroom as he seethed in anger, the envelope crumpling in his grasp. "This bitch got me fucked up."

Chill fell back into the chair, groaning as he reached for his phone and texted Shay:

Come get me.

He looked back at the open door and found Chantel arguing with someone out of his view. He stood up and headed out the door.

"... It was only a matter of time before he knew, Telly, don't you think?" He heard Rashad ask Chantel just as Jamal thundered out of the apartment as well, his eyes bloodshot and nostrils clouded with powder.

He glared around the front before waving the papers at Chantel, who now had Chill standing between the both of them.

"Parental rights for joint custody of Alani with Rashad? Dez's brother?! The fuck, Chantel?"

She jumped in fright as he tried to maneuver around Chill, who raised his hands to block his path. "Calm down, Mal. I don't wanna do this."

"Cuz, move the fuck outta my way! This doesn't concern you!" Jamal yelled, eyes wild with fury, but Chill still did not move.

"I'm not letting you touch her—"

Without warning, Jamal threw a punch at Chill, effectively connecting with his nose and forcing him to stumble backward. Blood streamed down Chill's nostrils as he groaned in his discomfort, but he stood his ground, glancing backward to find Rashad still beside Chantel. He felt rage quickly replace the pain he felt, but before he could react, Dez butted in.

"Fuck his ass up, Mal!" Dez urged from his spot by the stairs, his voice rising.

Chill turned and, without hesitation, landed a punch squarely on Dez's mouth, knocking him off his feet and stumbling down the first flight of stairs.

The pain in Chill's nose could not compare to the smugness he felt.

"I owed you that one, you *fucking* bitch!" Chill spat.

Rashad, seeing his brother down, rushed at Chill while his brother balled himself up in pain, kicking him hard in the stomach and taking everybody by surprise. Jamal stood back, fists clenched, torn between helping or just walking away. His eyes met Chantel's, which was brimmed with tears just as a gunshot rang out.

Chill felt goosebumps rise against his skin as he quickly checked himself for injury, his gaze returning to Rashad, who stood above him with a stunned expression on his face.

His eyes immediately went to his stomach, blood quickly seeping into his shirt and staining the fabric as he immediately clutched it.

The blood leaked through his fingers, and Rashad soon collapsed.

"Rashad?" Dez called from the landing, pulling himself up the stairs to his brother, whom he shook to get a reaction. "Rashad!" His voice broke as he rocked his brother over again. "Wake *up!*"

Chill turned to where the gunshot had come from to see Di'Vanni standing by the door with the gun still smoking in his hand, wide-eyed with fear.

"Di'..." Chill said softly, struggling to get up and make his way towards the boy. "It's okay... just drop the gun."

"I'm scared, Dad," Di'Vanni whispered, trembling as he let go of the gun, letting it fall.

Chill managed a small smile as he kicked the gun away. "There's nothing to be scared about, son... You didn't do anything wrong."

As he got close enough to hug Di'Vanni, the pressure immediately got to the boy, and he collapsed, hitting the ground with impact.

Chantel screamed and hurried to reach for him. "Di'!" She cradled him in her arms. "Baby… not now, please… Mal, please call an ambulance."

She looked up to see Jamal staring at the both of them with a blank look on his face before wiping his nose.

"… Son?"

His voice was cold, dry, and haunting as he tilted his head at them. Chill could see nothing behind his eyes, and he hated how much it freaked him out.

Dez, seizing the moment, fumbling to pull out his phone with one hand as the other applied pressure on his brother's stomach. "That's what I've been trying to tell your ass. Your cousin's a snake! I got it all on video—"

Another gunshot went off, and Chantel screamed.

Dez stilled, a bullet hole appearing in his forehead as he fell backward with a nasty *thump*.

"Jamal!" Chill yelled in disbelief. "What the hell are you doing? Your son needs *help!*"

Jamal barked a humorless laugh.

"My son?! When has that kid ever been mine?!" he yelled, waving the gun around. "Hell, when has *anything* ever been mine, Chill? You just have to take everything away from me. *Every fucking thing!*"

He frustratedly ran a hand through his hair.

"I wanted to be in the fucking Navy, but you took it from me. You made me a fucking *ex-convict*. You treated me like I was a fucking junkie. I

64

fell in love, but you couldn't stand it, could you? You had to take her and my kids like you've taken everything else, Cedric!"

Chill's gaze dulled as he watched Jamal break down.

"I hate you, you know?" he said, exhaling. "So much that I wanted you gone, but no, Kev just had to botch it and kill Nate instead. But you know what, cuz?"

Their eyes met, and Chill slowly shook his head when the gun was once again in his direction. "Mal, you ain't got the heart."

"I'll do you a solid..." he muttered, cocking the gun once more. "I'll send you to Nate. Pain-free."

Mal's glare darkened as he wordlessly shot Chill in the chest, watching as his cousin staggered back and fell with blood pouring from his mouth. Chantel's scream rang throughout as Chill held her hand, his mouth moving but still speechless. His grip was tight, and he seemed to want to hold Di'Vanni before eventually stilling.

He lay on the ground, eyes rolled back and staring at the sky completely motionlessly as Chantel turned to Jamal.

"You've lost your mind! You're fucking insane!"

"And I have a right to be. You two fucked up my entire life!" he retorted, seeing anger flash through her features.

"I fucking loved him before you came into the picture. I loved Chill all my life!"

Do you think I wouldn't notice that? Jamal thought as he turned the gun on himself. As much as he hated Chill, there was no way he was letting his cousin rot in hell without him. And besides, what else would he live for?

He could hear Chantel yell his name as he opened his mouth and then pulled the trigger.

It all went dark.

Made in the USA
Columbia, SC
08 October 2024

43966348R00041